TO

Hawke & Scout

FROM

David Hunt   N J Trammell

DATE

_____

A "SWEET WILLIE MCDUFFIE" BOOK

Willie Takes the High Road

WRITTEN BY DAVID HUNT

ILLUSTRATED BY NORMA JEANNE TRAMMELL

ISBN: 978-0-578-57140-9

THIS BOOK IS DEDICATED TO AMY.

Willie McDuffie is sitting on his front porch just like he does most mornings.
Suddenly, his ears perk up at the sound of someone yelling.

"Willeeee!!!" Willie takes off running through the grass.
The woman down the road hollers for Willie almost every day.

Willie runs extra fast because his friend,
Zoe, lives with the woman, and Willie loves Zoe!

Papa Dave always watches Willie when he visits Zoe, just to make sure that Willie is safe.

One day, as Willie trotted up the sidewalk on his way back home, he noticed Scout watching him from across the street.

Just as Willie walks back into his front yard,
he hears Scout bark,

"Hey, Fatso! You better be careful!!
If that tummy grows any bigger, you'll be dragging it on the ground!"

"What?" Willie thinks, "Did Scout just call me 'Fatso'?"
Willie asks Scout, "Are you talking to me?"

Scout snarls, "You know it's true!"
Willie turns quickly and runs to his house.

Willie's tail droops. He wonders, "Why was Scout barking about me like that? I thought he was my friend."

Then, Willie notices his sister Susie sitting on the porch.
"Susie, did you hear what Scout said?"

"Oh, don't listen to him," says Susie, he's just being a bully."
"What's a bully?" asks Willie.

"A bully is someone who makes fun of someone else.
They say cruel and mean things", answers Susie.

"But why would anyone act like that?" Willie sniffles.
He just couldn't understand.

"I think they do it because it makes them feel better to put others down.
The best thing you can do is just ignore him."

"No!" Willie said, "I've got a better idea. I'm going to get Brutus, the huge Great Dane up the street, to go scare Scout.

Brutus is as tall as a pony, so Scout better watch out!"

"What?" yelled Susie. "No way! That would only cause more trouble!
It wouldn't solve any problems, and then YOU you would be a bully.

Besides, everyone calls you SWEET Willie McDuffie'!"
You don't want to be a bully."

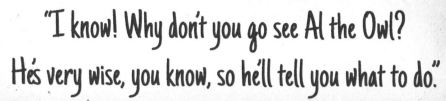

"I know! Why don't you go see Al the Owl?
He's very wise, you know, so he'll tell you what to do."

"Good idea," agreed Willie.

"I'll go see him right now, but I'll have to wake him up.
He sleeps all day so he can hunt all night."

Willie takes off running
toward the backyard fence,
which borders the edge of
the forest near Al's tree.

When he gets to the bottom of the tree, Willie howls.
"Al! Hello! Are you home?"

Al calls back sleepily, "Whooo are you?"

Willie replies, "It's me, Willie McDuffie!" Willie stretches his back and puts his paws on the base of the tree, and, sure enough, he sees Al perched on a branch.

"Al, I've got a problem, and I'm hoping you can help me figure out how to handle it." "I will try," Al said.

Willie tells Al what Scout said. When he finishes, he asks Al, "What should I do?"

Al put his wing to his cheek like he was thinking really hard. "Let me tell you a true story.

One day years ago, I was sitting in the veterinarian's office waiting to have my eyes checked. There was a long line of animals waiting to sign in."

"A young deer walked in. He had already signed in but had run back home to get a paper the doctor needed. He waved to the receptionist to let them know he had returned, but some turkey near the back of the line thought the deer was trying to break in line."

"The turkey angrily waddled over to the buck and started bullying him until the buck's back was against the wall.

He gobbled to the buck, "'Come with me outside! We'll settle this with a fight!'" The deer calmly looked at the turkey and said softly, "'I'm not going ANYWHERE with you.'"

"The turkey was totally stumped,

so he turned around and returned to his place in line."

"You see, Willie, you don't have to go anywhere with anybody. Just go your own way. Choose to follow your own road and walk away."

"You have been taught what is right or wrong, so take the HIGH ROAD."

Willie feels so excited about what he learned, he barks, "Thanks!" and sprints back home to tell Susie.

When he finishes telling Susie what Al had told him, she said, "Al the Owl was right. While you were gone, Scout came over and apologized. That sure beats fighting or trying to get even with Scout, doesn't it?"

Willie agreed, and he knew that he would always remember to—
TAKE THE HIGH ROAD.

THE END.

Listen to the "Sweet Willie McDuffie" Sing-Along:

facebook.com/davidhuntbooks

"Sweet Willie McDuffie" Sing-Along Song

V.1

They call me Sweet Willie McDuffie, I come from the county of York,

My daddy once visited Malta, and I was brought home by a stork,

They say that I'm Maltese and Yorkie, I think that is probably true,

'Cause I bark with a slight English accent, and Maltese girls all think I'm cute.

Cho.

Sweet Willie McDuffie, Sweet Willie McDuffie that's me,

No, I'm not Sweet Willie McAfferty, and I'm not Sweet Willie McFee,

There lots of Sweet Willie McSomethings, the confusion can sometimes get "ruff",

So if someone happens to ask you, just tell ém I'm Willie McDuffieeeeeeeeeeee.

V.2

They transplanted me here in Gergia, in the south of the U.S. of A,

With collards and grits and fried chicken and lots of big places to play,

So if you should ever come down here, I wish you would give me a call,

Just ask for Sweet Willie McDuffie, 'cause everyone else is named Y'aaaaaaaaaall!

Cho.

V.3

I guess that I'd better go home now, I hear someone calling my name,

I know that it must be my parents, and I always do what they say,

They take care of me and they love me, and I love them back just the same,

That's why they call me "Sweet" Willie, that is how I got my name!

Cho. (repeat with multiple voices)

Meet the Author, David Hunt.

David Hunt, a native of Georgia, is a retired educator. He has worked with students of every grade level, pre-k through twelfth. He spent the first half of his career in the classroom and the second half as a principal at an elementary school, a middle school and a high school. During his career, one of David's guiding principles was that every young person's problems, challenges and worries are just as strong and important to them as any problems, challenges and worries being faced by an adult. David has always been an animal lover. As he would take his dog Willie on trips to the veterinarian, David wrote a song about Willie (which is included in this book). This is the first, published story about Willie, and there are more to come. Each story teaches a lesson regarding coping mechanisms that the reader will, hopefully, at some time, employ.

Meet the Illustrator, Norma Jeanne Trammell.

Jeanne Trammell, sometimes known as Norma JEANNE, is a local artist in Middle Georgia. She works in watercolor, oil, pastels and acrylics and has traveled the world sketching and painting on location. Jeanne is a retired kindergarten teacher, an artist, book illustrator and art instructor. Her philosophy is "Art is not something apart from our lives. It is about love, adventure, therapy, humor and most of all a celebration of life!"
She can be reached On Facebook, Watercolors by NJ.

Made in the USA
Columbia, SC
19 June 2020